Wee Witches' Halloween

For my father, Godfrey
—J.S.

Copyright © 2002 by Jerry Smath.
All rights reserved. Published by Scholastic Inc.
SCHOLASTIC, CARTWHEEL BOOKS, and associated logos
are trademarks and/or registered trademarks of Scholastic Inc.

Library of Congress Cataloging-in-Publication Data

Smath, Jerry.
      Wee witches' Halloween / by Jerry Smath.
          p.   cm. (Read with me paperbacks)
      "Cartwheel Books."
      Summary: Although they have gone to Scaring School, four young witches have trouble making
anyone afraid of them on Halloween.
      ISBN 0-439-36740-9 (pbk)
      [1. Witches— Fiction. 2. Schools— Fiction. 3. Halloween— Fiction. 4. Stories in rhyme.] I. Title.
II. Series.
PZ8.3.S64 We 2002
[E]— dc21   2001049319

                        15   12/0

Printed in the U.S.A.   40
First printing, September 2002

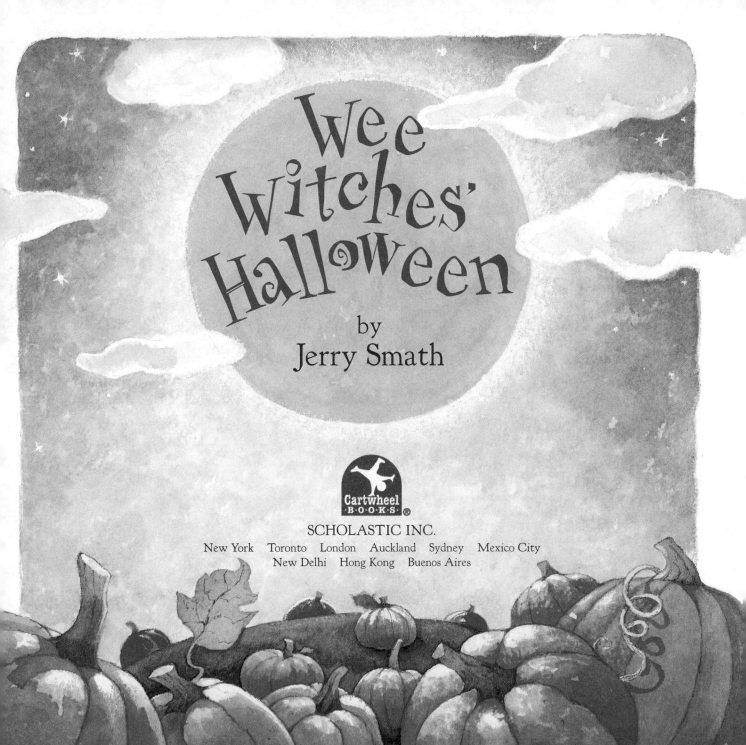

Wee Witches' Halloween

by
Jerry Smath

Cartwheel
·B·O·O·K·S·®

SCHOLASTIC INC.

New York   Toronto   London   Auckland   Sydney   Mexico City
New Delhi   Hong Kong   Buenos Aires

On Halloween, wee witches hatch

from pumpkins in this pumpkin patch.

Before their spree, there is one rule:

They first must go to Scaring School.

In class, the older witches teach

the younger ones just how to screech.

The lesson now is scaring frogs—

causing them to fall off logs.

Then each witch, with cat and broom,

must learn to fly from tomb to tomb.

The text on the diploma reads: DIPLOMA — I am a witch

When school is over, the witches are free

to scare us all on their Halloween spree.

From the air they spot a fair.

Perhaps there's someone there to scare!

All four scream, "BOO!"—but soon they find

that no one really seems to mind.

Next the screeching witches raid

a passing Halloween parade.

They try to frighten ghosts and bats

and moms and dads in silly hats.

But their screams, it seems, don't turn a head—

and the witches win first prize instead!

And when they find they cannot scare,
it's much too much for them to bear.

About to leave in their defeat,
they hear the kids shout, "Trick-or-treat!"

So they decide, with one last try,

to scare some kids and make them cry.

Now the screaming witchy team,
regrets that they have been so mean…

for when they scream their biggest "BOO!"

the kids just laugh and scream **Boo** too!